Hula Lullaby

erin eitter kono

 LITTLE, BROWN AND COMPANY
New York · Boston

For Kirk

With special thanks to Namaka, my muse;

and Halau Keali`i O Nalani

Little, Brown and Company
Time Warner Book Group
1271 Avenue of the Americas, New York, NY 10020
Visit our Web site at www.lb-kids.com

First Edition

Library of Congress Cataloging-in-Publication Data

Kono, Erin Eitter.
Hula lullaby / Erin Eitter Kono.—1st ed.
p. cm.
Summary: Against the backdrop of a beautiful Hawaiian landscape, a young girl cuddles and sleeps in her mother's lap.
ISBN 0-316-73591-4
[1. Mother and child—Fiction. 2. Bedtime—Fiction. 3. Hawaii—Fiction. 4. Stories in rhyme.] I. Title.

PZ8.3.K8415Hu 2005
[E]—dc22   2004010270

10 9 8 7 6 5 4 3 2 1

TWP

Printed in Singapore

The illustrations for this book were done in acrylic and pencil on Arches Aquarelle Cold Press paper.
The text was set in Maiandra, and the display type is Cepo.

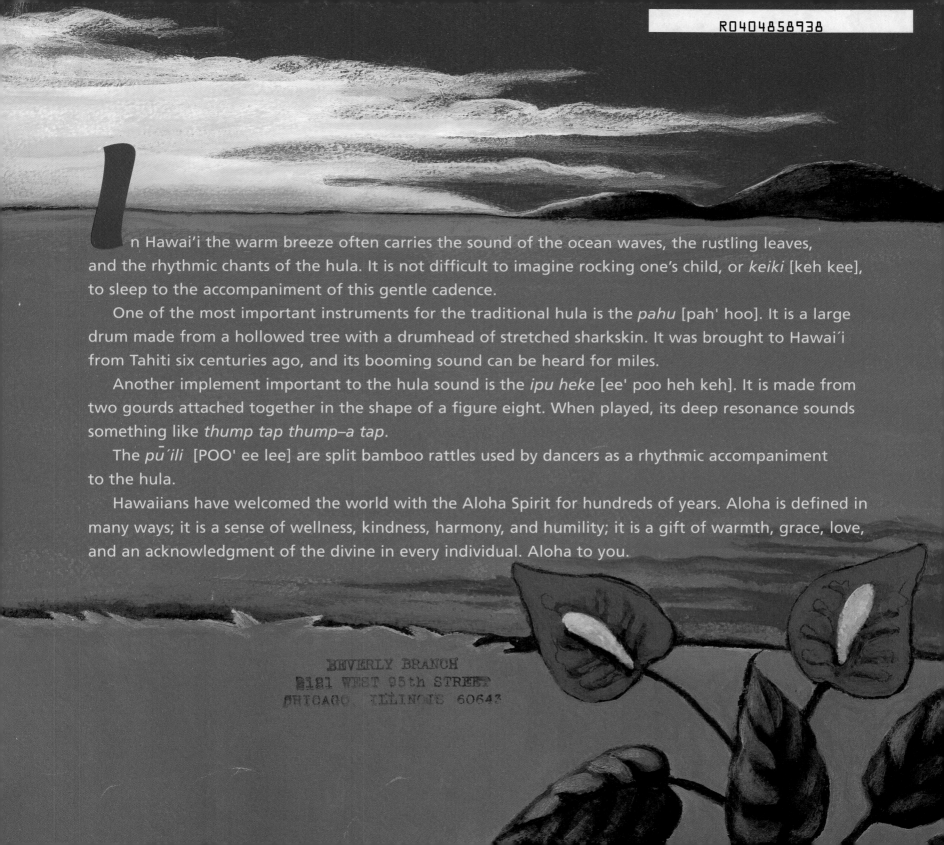

In Hawai'i the warm breeze often carries the sound of the ocean waves, the rustling leaves, and the rhythmic chants of the hula. It is not difficult to imagine rocking one's child, or *keiki* [keh kee], to sleep to the accompaniment of this gentle cadence.

One of the most important instruments for the traditional hula is the *pahu* [pah' hoo]. It is a large drum made from a hollowed tree with a drumhead of stretched sharkskin. It was brought to Hawai'i from Tahiti six centuries ago, and its booming sound can be heard for miles.

Another implement important to the hula sound is the *ipu heke* [ee' poo heh keh]. It is made from two gourds attached together in the shape of a figure eight. When played, its deep resonance sounds something like *thump tap thump–a tap.*

The *pūʻili* [POO' ee lee] are split bamboo rattles used by dancers as a rhythmic accompaniment to the hula.

Hawaiians have welcomed the world with the Aloha Spirit for hundreds of years. Aloha is defined in many ways; it is a sense of wellness, kindness, harmony, and humility; it is a gift of warmth, grace, love, and an acknowledgment of the divine in every individual. Aloha to you.

Come little keiki
Crawl into my lap

Listen to the ipu
Thump tap thump-a tap

See the fire's glow
Toss its golden light

Feel the ocean's breeze
Warm against your hair

Watch as hula hands
Sway gently in the air

Come little keiki
Nestle in my lap

Listen to the ipu
Thump tap thump-a tap

Hear the crashing waves
Reach the lava shore

Drummers chant the ancient tales
Of history and lore

See the moon rise high
To spread its silver glow

Watch as ti leaf skirts

Sway gently to and fro

Come little keiki

Snuggle in my lap

Listen to the ipu
Thump tap thump-a tap

Mountain peaks enfold you
In their kind embrace

Dancers move their feet
To the pahu's rhythmic pace

Birds rustle in the brush

Fish swim in the sea

The Dancers tap in time
With their pū´ili

Come little keiki
Sleep here in my lap

Listen to the ipu
Thump tap thump-a tap

The scent of tropic blooms
Perfumes the darkened sky

Music rocks you lightly
With its hula lullaby

Below us Mother Earth lies still
Above us palm trees sway

Hawai´i sends you off to sleep
In the Aloha way

Come little keiki
Dream sweetly in my lap

Listen to the ipu
Thump tap thump-a tap